Once upon a time...

Front cover illustrated by Judy Nostrant

Back cover and title page illustrations by Jane Maday

Contributing Writers:
Dorothea Goldenburg
Bette Killian

Book Illustrations by
Jane Maday
Jim Salvati
Joe Spencer
Gary Torrisi
Phil Wilson

Louis Weber, C.E.O., Publications International, Ltd.
7373 North Cicero Avenue, Lincolnwood, Illinois 60712

Ground Floor, 59 Gloucester Place, London W1U 8JJ

Customer Service: 1-800-595-8484 or customer_service@pilbooks.com

www.pilbooks.com

Manufactured in China

8 7 6 5 4 3 2 1

ISBN-13: 978-1-4127-8376-7

ISBN-10: 1-4127-8376-3

Favorite Children's Stories

pi kids® publications international, ltd.

Contents

Beauty and the Beast

In a far-away country lived a rich merchant with his three lovely daughters, Bliss, Blossom, and Beauty. They lived comfortably in a large house with many servants. One day, however, the merchant lost all his ships to storms at sea. The family could no longer afford its fine house or servants, so the merchant and his daughters moved to a small cottage.

At first, Bliss and Blossom were unhappy. They complained about the luxuries they had lost and the work they now had to do. But Beauty said, "Crying will not make things better. We must learn to be happy here."

She worked every day, cleaning, cooking, and gardening, and she helped her sisters learn to enjoy their new life. The merchant was proud of all three girls, but especially of Beauty.

One day, the merchant heard that a ship he owned had returned safely, and he prepared for the long journey to the port. Each daughter wished him a safe journey, and the merchant promised to bring back gifts. Bliss and Blossom wanted ball gowns and fine jewelry.

"What would you like, Beauty?" the merchant asked.

"A rose," said Beauty, "just a lovely rose."

When the merchant reached the port, he learned that his cargo of fine silk had been ruined by seawater that had leaked into the ship. He was just as poor as before.

The merchant rode sadly home, passing through a part of the woods that he had never traveled before. As night fell, he began to hear soft rustling sounds behind him and eerie howls in the distance. Suddenly, a raging storm blew up, and he became lost in a deep, swirling mist of snow.

The merchant pressed bravely on, but he soon realized that he would have to stop for the night. In the distance, he saw a yellow light that seemed to cut through the blizzard. He struggled toward it, hoping that he would find a small village or a tiny hut where he could sit out the storm. He stepped into a clearing—and came upon the most magnificent palace he had ever seen!

The merchant tied his horse to the gate and went inside. He could not find the owner of the castle, but he did discover an inviting fire, a wonderful meal, and a soft, warm bed.

The next morning, the merchant explored the palace grounds. Even though it was winter, the garden was filled with colorful flowers of all kinds. He came upon a lovely rose bush and, remembering Beauty's request, decided to pick one for her. As he broke the stem of the flower, the air was filled with a terrible roar, and a huge beast appeared as if from nowhere.

"Thief! Robber!" the Beast bellowed. "I offered you food and shelter, and you stole from me! For this I must put you in the dungeon."

The merchant begged the Beast to let him take the rose to Beauty and see his daughters one last time. Touched by the man's love for his family, the Beast gave him a magic ring to take him from the castle to his home, and the merchant promised to return and accept his punishment. He arrived home and told his daughters what had happened.

"Must you go, Father?" asked Bliss. "We will miss you so."

"It is only a beast," protested Blossom. "Do you have to keep a promise to such a creature?"

"I gave my word!" said the merchant.

Beauty said nothing, but as soon as all were asleep, she took the magic ring and used it to carry her to the castle of the Beast, knowing that her father could not follow her.

Beauty told the Beast that she wanted to take her father's place. "When he plucked the rose, he was only doing what I had asked," she explained. "I should be the one to stay here with you."

Again, the Beast was moved, and he agreed. "You will not stay as a prisoner, but as my guest."

The Beast worked hard to make Beauty happy. He saw that she had beautiful clothes, delicious meals, and fresh flowers from the garden. Every evening they would have dinner together and spend many hours talking. The Beast soon fell in love with Beauty. He often thought of telling her, but he was ashamed of his frightful appearance and so never spoke of his feelings.

In time, Beauty came to care for the Beast very much. She admired the pride he took in his garden, and she loved the gentle way he tended to the animals on the palace grounds. But she also missed her father and sisters, and one day she asked if she might visit them.

"Very well," said the Beast, giving her the magic ring. "But I can let you go for only ten days. At the end of the tenth day, you must return."

Beauty went home, and her family was overjoyed to see her. When the time came for her to return to the Beast, she could not bear to leave. She decided to stay one more day.

As Beauty slept that night, she dreamed that the Beast was lying helpless in his garden. He seemed to be dying. She was so frightened by the dream that the next morning she used the ring to return to the palace. All was strangely quiet.

She called out but heard no answer. She rushed to the garden and found the Beast lying just as she had seen him in her dream.

"Oh, Beast, don't die!" she cried. "You are so kind, and I do love you! You are ugly, but your goodness is easy to see!"

With Beauty's words, the Beast changed into a handsome prince.

"An old fairy turned me into a beast to teach me a lesson," said the Prince. "I was often cruel to animals that I thought ugly. The spell would be broken only when someone grew to love me in spite of the way I looked."

The Prince and Beauty were married at once. Her father, her sisters, and all the people who belonged to the Prince's court came to celebrate the wedding.

No longer a beast in either body or spirit, the Prince loved Beauty with all his heart and provided for her and her family for the rest of their days.

Rapunzel

John and his wife Nell lived in a pleasant cottage in a small village. More than anything, they wished for a child. Next door lived a wicked witch named Helga. She had a house with a big garden. Helga wished for a child, too.

One day, Nell had a sign that she would have a baby. That same day, she saw some rapunzel lettuce growing in the witch's garden. It looked so green and fresh. Nell cried, "I must have some of that lettuce!"

John loved her so much that he risked picking some of the lettuce for her.

"How dare you steal my rapunzel!" the witch screamed when she came upon him. "You will pay dearly for this!"

John explained about his wife's hunger for the lettuce.

Unappeased, Helga said, "Very well, take all the lettuce you like, but when the baby is born, it will be mine."

John was so shaken that he agreed. Nell ate a very great deal of rapunzel lettuce, and in time a beautiful little girl was born. She had blue eyes and golden hair. Her parents loved her at once.

The next day, Helga came to claim the child as her own. True to his word, John sadly let the witch take the child away. The old hag named her Rapunzel and spirited the baby away to a distant land.

Rapunzel's thick golden hair grew fast and long. Helga loved to show off the beautiful child.

One evening when Rapunzel was twelve years old, Helga used her powers to call the great Raven of the North. She told him to carry Rapunzel away to a high tower in a forest. The Raven did as he was told, and Helga was waiting when they arrived. She imprisoned Rapunzel in the tower, which had no doors or stairs and only one chamber at the top.

Rapunzel was frightened when the witch went away. But the Raven stayed through the first night and made soft sounds to soothe her. He felt sorry for Rapunzel, but he had no powers of his own. He could not defy Helga's will.

The next morning, Rapunzel heard Helga calling from outside the tower:

"Rapunzel, Rapunzel, let down your hair."

Rapunzel wound her long tresses around a hook next to the window and let down her hair. It looked like spun gold. Helga caught up the strands and climbed the side of the tower. She stayed with Rapunzel only a short time, bringing food and water.

Every morning, Helga came and called to Rapunzel, and every morning Rapunzel let down her long hair. But Rapunzel was still lonely. She made friends with the birds who flew by her window, and they taught her to sing beautifully. She spent many hours singing to the forest.

The rabbits, the foxes, the deer—even the bears and the wolves—loved to hear Rapunzel singing. They stopped wherever they were in the forest and listened.

On some days, the squirrels or a raccoon might climb up the tower wall and bring Rapunzel some nuts or a juicy apple.

A little bluebird came every morning to perch on Rapunzel's windowsill. Rapunzel named her Sky because the bird was as blue as the heavens and as happy as a little sunbeam. Every morning, Sky sang with Rapunzel and then flew away just as Helga approached the tower.

After Rapunzel had been in the tower for a long, long time, a handsome prince came riding through the forest on a mission for his father, the King. Suddenly, he heard a beautiful voice singing somewhere among the trees. He guided his horse toward the enchanting sound. When he got closer, the singing stopped and a harsh voice called:

"Rapunzel, Rapunzel, let down your hair."

The Prince was amazed to see the beautiful long hair and the ugly witch climbing up it. He wanted to hear the girl sing again, but the witch stayed. The Prince vowed that he would return one day and so rode on to carry out his royal task.

As the Prince rode back through the forest on his way home, he came again to the tower. All was quiet. He walked to the foot of the tower and called, as he had heard Helga call:

"Rapunzel, Rapunzel, let down your hair."

At once, Rapunzel came to the window, but she hesitated because the voice was strange. When she saw the Prince, she let down her hair and the Prince climbed swiftly to her window.

"Sing for me!" he begged her. Rapunzel was so happy that she sang more sweetly than ever before.

Every day after that, the Prince climbed up to see Rapunzel. And every day she sang for him.

One day, Helga arrived at the tower earlier than usual. As she came near, she heard Rapunzel singing. The song was so sweet that Helga knew something had happened.

She crept close to the tower and watched. Soon she saw Rapunzel tell the Prince good-bye. She watched him climb down from the tower on the golden hair, then ride away through the forest.

"Someone has tricked me!" Helga screeched.

She dashed home without leaving the food and water for Rapunzel. Back in her own cottage, she stormed and stomped and shrieked that someone was trying to steal her own, beautiful daughter!

When evening came, Helga called forth all her powers and summoned the great Raven of the North.

"Take them both!" commanded Helga. "Fly them to the poorest, most miserable kingdom on earth and leave them there! Then they will be unhappy all their lives!"

As the Raven reached the tower, he saw Rapunzel and the Prince escaping from the tower on the girl's tresses. She had cut off her hair and tied it to the window hook. The Raven grasped the two in his claws and started for the far country. The two held each other close, and Rapunzel—still happy to be with her Prince—began to sing.

The music that had charmed and enchanted the creatures of the forest when Rapunzel was trapped in the tower now stirred the Raven's heart. The song seemed to say to him that, no matter how difficult life could be, all that mattered was being with the ones we love. The music and words gave the great black bird the strength to disobey Helga's orders.

Instead of taking them to a barren kingdom, the Raven flew Rapunzel and the Prince straight to the girl's humble cottage.

At the sound of the great wings flapping, Rapunzel's parents, John and Nell, came outside. To their surprise and delight, they saw their beautiful child once again.

The Prince then asked John for his daughter's hand in marriage. The proud father gladly gave the young couple his heartiest blessing.

Soon after, the Prince and Rapunzel were married in a splendid ceremony. They took Rapunzel's parents with them to live in the King's castle, far, far away.

The wicked witch, who did not know that the Raven had defied her, lived out her days in loneliness and was never heard from again.

Aladdin

Aladdin was a poor boy who lived in a small house just outside the city. He made his living by gathering sticks and selling them for kindling at the market.

One day, he loaded a bundle of sticks on his back and walked to the city. Amir, his pet mongoose, rode on his shoulder, looking alertly around him. There were many wondrous sights to see in the city.

In the midst of the great, bustling crowd in the marketplace that day, a voice suddenly cried out, "Make way! Make way! The Sultan's daughter, Princess Lylah, is coming through!"

The Princess rode on a splendid white horse with her royal court around her. Aladdin pushed to the front of the crowd to get a glimpse of her. She was beautiful!

Amir saw her, too, and began chattering so loudly that the Princess turned and smiled at him and his master. Aladdin's heart filled with love for her.

Standing in the crowd next to Aladdin was a clever magician named Rasheed. He looked Aladdin up and down and remarked, "Young man, I could use your help. I will give you a gold coin if you do a simple task for me."

Aladdin followed Rasheed into the desert. They walked a long way until they came to a mountainous area.

"Here," said Rasheed, pointing to a small opening in the mountainside. "I cannot fit through the entrance to the cave, but I am sure that you can. Climb down into the cave and bring me the bronze lamp you find there. And hurry!"

Aladdin slid into the cave. There he found precious jewels and coins heaped in piles—and the lamp in a corner. He was about to hand it out to the magician when Amir chattered loudly and jerked his sleeve.

"Give it to me!" shrieked the magician, but Aladdin refused.

Rasheed was so angry that he wedged a heavy rock in the mouth of the cave, blocking the hole, and left. Aladdin filled his pockets with as many precious stones as he could carry, then with the lamp on his lap he sat down to ponder his plight. Amir ran 'round and 'round, looking for a way out, but there was none. Aladdin began to weep.

His tears rolled down onto the lamp, and Aladdin rubbed them away. As he did, a huge genie in a cloud of green smoke appeared.

"What is your desire, Master? Your wish is my command," the genie thundered.

Aladdin cried, "Get us out of here!"

No sooner had Aladdin spoken than he and Amir were outside the cave. He still clutched the bronze lamp. He felt in his pockets to make sure that he still had the precious jewels.

Back home again, Aladdin felt hungry. He rubbed the lamp and asked the genie to bring him food. Immediately, his table was spread with a feast fit for the Sultan, all served on fine plates and crockery. The food was delicious, but Aladdin could not eat much. His heart was aching for the Sultan's beautiful daughter, Lylah.

He asked the genie to dress him in royal clothes and give him a noble horse. Then Aladdin rode to the Sultan's palace. In a leather pouch, he carried Amir and the precious stones from the desert cave.

The Sultan's palace was huge and richly appointed. Aladdin trembled at the sight, but his love for the Princess calmed him.

"Sire," he said, kneeling before the Sultan, "I bring you these humble jewels and ask your daughter's hand in marriage."

The Sultan had never before seen such rich jewels. He thought Aladdin must be the son of a powerful sultan from another country. So he agreed to give him Princess Lylah as his wife.

Lylah was pleased that Aladdin had asked for her hand, for she thought him a kind and handsome young man.

Aladdin and the Princess were married, and the genie built them a palace even more beautiful than the Sultan's. Aladdin and the Princess were happy there until the day Rasheed learned about what had happened. The magician knew that the young husband had his magic lamp.

He hurried to a shop and bought a dozen shiny bronze lamps. One day when Aladdin was not home, Rasheed dressed as a peddler and brought the lamps to the palace.

"New lamps for old," he whined, "new lamps for old!" The Princess, remembering Aladdin's battered old lamp, thought to surprise him with a new one. The sly magician traded one of his shiny lamps for the magic one. Soon he summoned the genie.

"Build me a splendid palace in another city," Rasheed commanded, "and bring me Princess Lylah."

It was done at once.

Aladdin returned to his palace to find that his beloved wife was gone. Poor Aladdin! His heart was broken. But Amir slipped away and began to look for her.

For many days, the little mongoose searched. At last, hungry and exhausted, he came to Rasheed's palace. There he found Princess Lylah, sobbing for Aladdin. When Amir crept into her lap, she kissed him and tied her silk hair ribbon around his neck.

The brave little mongoose hurried back to his master. When Aladdin saw the scarf, he followed Amir to Rasheed's palace. There, while the wicked magician was sleeping, they found the magic lamp and, in a wink, the genie spirited Aladdin, Princess Lylah, and Amir back to their home.

When the Sultan heard the story, he was very angry. He banished the evil Rasheed, who was never heard from again.

Aladdin and the beautiful Lylah lived happily after that. They raised a large family, and the favorite playmates of their many children and grandchildren were several generations of mongoose—the offspring of the faithful Amir!

The Sleeping Beauty

Long ago, a wise and loving king and queen ruled a distant land. They were very happy, but still they wished every day for a child to share their joy.

One summer's day, the King and Queen went down to the garden pond where it was cool. All around the water's edge were long cattails and beautiful water lilies. As the Queen looked into the water, a large green frog jumped out.

The frog looked up at the royal pair and said, "My King and Queen, you have ruled with fairness and kindness, and for that I will grant your wish. Before the year has passed, you will have the child you long for." With a great splash, the frog disappeared into the water.

Just as the frog had promised, a beautiful baby girl was born, and the King and Queen ordered a celebration to welcome their daughter, whom they named Rosamond.

A great feast was prepared, the likes of which the kingdom had never seen. The castle was decorated from top to bottom with streamers in blue, green, and gold. Court musicians wrote new songs to be played in the Princess's honor. Invitations were prepared for nobility, landowners, artisans, shopkeepers, peasants, and the thirteen fairies of the kingdom—everyone in the land was asked to come.

Well, almost everyone, for in the excitement and flurry, a mistake was made. One invitation was mislaid, and that simple mistake was to change Rosamond's life.

At the height of the festivities, the fairies gave Rosamond a special gift. One by one they approached the child and offered her a magical promise: As she grew in size, she would also grow in goodness. Just as the twelfth fairy was about to present her gift, Mordra, the last and most powerful of all the fairies, stormed in. It was her invitation that had been misplaced.

Mordra shouted furiously, "You have insulted me, so you will suffer! Before your precious Rosamond reaches her sixteenth year, she will prick her finger on a spinning wheel spindle and die!"

The twelfth fairy rushed to Rosamond's cradle. "My gift is this, sweet child," she proclaimed. "You shall not die, but rather fall into a deep sleep that will be ended by the promise of true love."

Years passed, and each day Rosamond grew to be more wonderful, just as the fairies had promised. She was sweet and gentle and quite beautiful.

Unlike even the simplest child in the kingdom, though, Rosamond did not know what a spinning wheel was, for she had never seen one. The King and Queen had long ago ordered that they all be removed from the castle.

On the eve of her sixteenth birthday, Rosamond was exploring the palace, as she was accustomed to doing, and came upon a staircase that went up an old tower. In a small room at the top sat a gentle-looking old woman at a spinning wheel, spinning the most delicate, shimmering thread Rosamond had ever seen.

"Good day," said the polite Rosamond. "Whatever are you doing?"

"I am just spinning," replied the woman with a sly smile. Rosamond did not realize that the hag was really Mordra, nor did she realize the danger she was in. Curious, she reached out to touch the wheel and begged, "Oh, please let me try!"

In that instant, Mordra's evil wish was fulfilled. Rosamond pricked her finger on the spindle and spilled a single drop of blood. As the wicked fairy laughed, Rosamond slumped to the ground. She was not dead, as Mordra had hoped, but lay in an enchanted sleep.

As a part of the twelfth fairy's spell, a deep sleep also fell over the whole castle. The horses in the barn, the kittens in the courtyard, the pigeons on the rooftops, all nodded off right where they were. The cook fell asleep as he stirred the big pot of soup on the hearth, and the guards all snored loudly at their posts. Even the King and Queen slept, upright and proper, as they sat on their thrones.

Mordra, angry that her plan had been thwarted, caused a thick, tangled hedge of razor-sharp thorns to surround the castle.

"Let the promise of true love pass through that!" she cackled.

From village to village, stories were told of the fairies' placing Rosamond on a special bed as she lay in magical slumber.

Many young men tried to reach Rosamond, but none could pass the thorny hedge. One day, a prince from a far-away land heard the story of the Sleeping Beauty. Prince Evan was a bold and adventurous young man, and something about the story aroused his curiosity. He did not know why, but he felt sure that he must find this princess, and he set off at once.

After many days of hard riding, Evan came to the thorny hedge. As he reached out to push away a branch, flowers burst forth from every part of the hedge, and the branches parted to make a path to the castle.

Evan rushed into the courtyard. To his amazement, every living thing in the castle was fast asleep. Over the purring kittens, around the snoring guards, past the sleeping King and Queen, and up the tower stairs he ran. At the top, he found Rosamond asleep on her bed.

Dazzled by Rosamond's beauty, Evan knelt down and gently kissed the girl's cheek. Rosamond's eyes opened, and the first thing she saw was the face of the Prince.

"You have broken the spell," she said, "and in you I see the promise of true love."

The two walked back through the castle, and, as if by magic, life began to stir about them once again. The kittens stretched and yawned. The horses rose clumsily, then whinnied and switched their tails. The pigeons began cooing and flapping their wings. The cook resumed stirring his soup, while the guards stopped snoring and stood at attention.

The King and Queen awoke to find Rosamond and Evan standing before them. The twelfth fairy's gift had indeed come to pass.

Rosamond and Evan were wed soon after, and the young couple departed for the Prince's homeland, where they lived happily ever after.

Cinderella

Far across the ocean in a tiny village, an old gentleman lived with his young, beautiful daughter. A few years after his wife died he married a woman with two daughters, hoping to find someone kind to care for his own daughter. His new wife, however, turned out to be selfish and cruel.

The two sisters were just like their mother, vain and rude. They would primp at their mirror and find fault with everyone else. The old man's daughter was just the opposite. She was beautiful, kind, and good, and she loved animals.

One terrible winter, the old gentleman became ill and died, leaving his daughter alone with a selfish stepmother and two wicked stepsisters.

The stepsisters were mean and took pleasure in teasing the poor girl. "Do you think that we would play with you?" jeered Capricia, delighted to see her cry.

Away went her lovely clothes. Instead, they gave her torn dresses. "Just see how pretty our well-dressed girl is now," Agatha teased.

The stepsisters ordered her to do all the cleaning, cooking, and laundering. They had soft beds with fluffy pillows and blankets, but when the girl lay down to sleep, she had only a hard bed of straw and had to warm herself in a corner close to the fireplace.

Because she was so often covered with soot and cinders from the hearth, the girl was called Cinderella by her malicious stepsisters.

One day, the King sent invitations to a wonderful ball at the palace. Every girl was invited to meet the Prince. He was to dance with all the ladies and then, it was hoped, choose a bride.

When the stepsisters received the invitation, they were thrilled. "Quickly, help us get ready for the ball!" they commanded. Cinderella washed and ironed the dresses and helped the stepsisters choose the prettiest ribbons for their hair.

When the stepsisters were ready, Cinderella asked her stepmother if she could go, too. "Why, Cinderella!" came the sneering answer. "You have no clothes and are covered with tatters and dirt. We would be ashamed of you!" And with a laugh, the vicious stepmother and stepsisters were gone.

Cinderella burst into tears. "Oh, how I wish I could go, too!" she wailed. "If only I had a fairy godmother who could make wishes come true!" Instantly, in a cloud of silver dust, there appeared a prim, gray-haired lady carrying a magic wand—a fairy godmother!

"Well, then!" she said. "Here I am. Now let's get down to business!" She told Cinderella to bring her a large pumpkin, six gray mice, a fat whiskered rat, and two slender lizards.

With a dip and a swirl of the Fairy Godmother's magic wand, the pumpkin became a coach, the mice became horses, the rat a jolly coachman with a big mustache, and the lizards fancy footmen. For the finish, Cinderella's torn dress was transformed into a satin gown. On her dainty feet were sparkling glass slippers.

"Now, mind you're home before midnight, Cinderella!" warned the Fairy Godmother. "At the stroke of twelve, everything will disappear. Your coach will become a pumpkin again, and your clothes will return to rags!"

Cinderella nodded and climbed into the magnificent coach. When she arrived at the palace, the townspeople were curious to know who the mysterious beauty was. Even her stepmother and stepsisters did not recognize her.

The Prince rushed to welcome her and instantly fell in love. He danced every dance with Cinderella and would dance with no other. Everyone could see that the Prince and the mysterious lady had fallen in love.

Cinderella was so happy and excited that she forgot about the passing time. When she heard the palace clock begin to strike twelve, Cinderella rushed out the door and down the steps as quickly as her little feet could carry her. She never even turned around to wave good-bye to the Prince.

In her hurry, Cinderella did not notice that she had lost one of the glass slippers at the bottom of the palace staircase. All she could think of was getting home before everything disappeared into thin air.

As the coach hurried away from the palace, Cinderella felt her clothes changing into rags. The horses became mice again, the coachman ran away as a fat rat, the footmen slinked away as lizards, and a bruised and dirty pumpkin sat in the middle of the road.

When the stepmother and her daughters returned home from the ball, they found Cinderella asleep by the fire. She stretched her arms, rubbed her eyes, and asked them to tell her all about the the wonderful ball.

They told her about the handsome Prince and the beautiful woman who had arrived in a magnificent coach. Everyone at the ball had admired her satin dress and sparkling glass slippers. Now the Prince was searching to find the lady whose foot fit the lost shoe.

As Cinderella listened to the story, she smiled and gently patted her apron pocket. Deep inside was the other glass slipper, which her Fairy Godmother had let her keep.

The news spread throughout the village. The Prince, who had sunk into a melancholy mood following the ball, was now his energetic self again. He had begun searching for the lady whose foot fit the glass slipper, vowing that none other than she would be his wife.

When the Prince came to Cinderella's house, Capricia and Agatha rushed to try on the shoe. With a push and a squeeze, each one tried to make her foot fit the delicate slipper. Try as they might, their feet were just too big.

Cinderella washed her hands and face, stepped out of the kitchen, and said softly, "I would like to try, if I may." The stepmother and stepsisters howled with laughter. "Don't be ridiculous, Cinderella, it couldn't be you!" they said.

Cinderella curtsied to the Prince and sat down to try on the slipper. Her slender foot slid into it easily. She then drew the second shoe out of her apron pocket and put that one on as well. At that moment, the Fairy Godmother reappeared and waved her magic wand over the girl.

"Begone, you tattered clothing, good only for a scullery maid!" she declared. "Let my deserving godchild be dressed as splendidly as a princess!"

Instantly, Cinderella's shabby dress became the satin gown she had danced in at the palace. Her stepmother and stepsisters were flabbergasted! Though they didn't want to believe it, they realized that the mysterious lady at the ball was none other than their own overworked Cinderella. Now, they deeply regretted having treated her so poorly.

The handsome Prince also recognized Cinderella as his beautiful dancing partner. "This is my bride!" he shouted with joy. "I feared I would never find you! Why ever did you leave at the stroke of twelve?"

"I am sincerely sorry for leaving you on the palace steps," said Cinderella, "but the story of why I left in such haste would take too long."

"Too long?" cried the Prince. "On the contrary, my beloved, we have all the time in the world!"

On the off chance that he might find the lady he was looking for, the Prince had for several days carried with him a beautiful diamond ring, which he now slipped on Cinderella's finger. "Please say you will marry me!" he urged. Cinderella accepted at once.

In a few days' time, the Prince and Cinderella were married in a magnificent palace ceremony, the likes of which the kingdom had not seen for many a year. The young couple lived happily ever after.

As for the vain and selfish stepmother and her unpleasant daughters, well, they did not live quite as happily. They were never again invited to the palace, and the daughters spent their lives as lonely spinsters.

The Princess and the Pea

Andre was a most handsome prince. He was also the bravest, the strongest, and the kindest young man in living memory. When he came of age to be married, the King and Queen determined that a princess should be his bride.

"I will search for a *real* princess," Andre insisted. "A real princess has genteel manners, a kind and merry nature, and a caring heart. Beauty is not the most important thing."

"And a *real* princess is just what you deserve," said the Queen. The King promised to help his son find such a woman.

The King and the young Prince set out on their royal steeds. They traveled around the country to find a *real* princess, asking at all the villages and all the splendid palaces.

They found many beautiful young maidens. All of them thought Prince Andre so handsome that they wanted to marry him. Ambitious parents were also eager to have their daughters make such an important royal match.

But none was the *real* princess that Andre longed for. Some did not have gentle enough manners, and some had harsh voices. Some were too pushy or unloving— in other words, ill-natured.

Finally, the King and Prince Andre had to return home. The Prince was very sad: He had had such hopes of finding a real princess!

The Royal Cook tried to cheer him up. He made his favorite dish of lamb and dumplings. But Prince Andre just shook his handsome head. The Royal Jester tried to make him laugh with the most amusing stories he knew, but Prince Andre only grew sadder and more quiet.

The Royal Maids fitted his bed with his favorite silken sheets, but Prince Andre did not sleep well.

One night, there was a terrible storm throughout the kingdom. The rain poured down in torrents. Thunder boomed, and lightning forked through the sky. At the pitch of the storm there came a knock at the palace gate. The King opened it to find a princess standing there. She was drenched, and rain streamed from her hair and ran out her shoes.

"Good evening, Your Majesty," she said politely. "I am a *real* princess, and I have come to marry your son." The King led her into the great hall to let her dry herself before the fire.

Prince Andre thought she was lovely, and entirely well-mannered, but still he wondered whether she was a *real* princess. Why had she gone out in such a storm, all alone?

When she was dry again, the Princess told her story. Her name was Elaine, and she had come from a far kingdom. When she had heard about Prince Andre, she asked her father's leave to come to his castle.

"For I know that I am a *real* princess," she said.

Her father had sent her in a royal carriage with guards. During the storm, lightning had struck a tree near the carriage. The horses had been so frightened that they bolted and ran away into the forest. The guards ran after the horses, telling Princess Elaine to stay with the carriage. But she was anxious to see the Prince, so she came on foot alone.

"A real princess does not give up," she said, "and I am a *real* princess!"

"We shall see," said the Queen. Prince Andre and the King thought this maiden should be a true princess, but the Queen said they should make sure. She went into the bedroom with two servants and took all the sheets and blankets off the bed. Then she laid a dried pea in the middle of the bed. Next, they took twenty mattresses and placed them on top of the pea. Finally, they put twenty feather beds on top of the mattresses.

"This is where you will sleep tonight," the Queen told the Princess.

Princess Elaine smiled, thanked the King and Queen for their kindness, and climbed onto the bed.

The Queen did not sleep well. Many times she woke and slipped into the Princess's bedroom to see if she was sleeping in the high bed. The Princess was asleep, but the Queen noticed that she seemed to toss and turn.

Prince Andre also slept badly. He kept wondering if this beautiful girl was a *real* princess. He hoped she was because he thought he loved her already.

The King slept badly because he wondered about Elaine, too. He did not know what to do if she turned out not to be a true princess.

The next morning, Princess Elaine dressed and came to breakfast.

"Did you sleep well last night, dear?" asked the Queen.

"Yes, Your Majesty," said the Princess. "Except that. . . . Oh, I'm sure I just imagined this. I must have dreamed of rocks beneath me, bruising me black and blue. And yet, this morning, I found a bruise on my back."

"Ah," thought the Queen. "She felt the pea through twenty mattresses and twenty feather beds. No one but a *real* princess could have such tender skin!"

Prince Andre was overjoyed, and the King and Queen were very happy, too. Prince Andre knelt before the beautiful princess. "Will you be my wife?" he begged her.

"Indeed I will!" said Princess Elaine.

The King opened a golden chest filled with bright jewels. "For my royal daughter-in-law," he said.

The Queen gave her a motherly embrace, and Prince Andre opened a velvet box to give her a magnificent golden ring with diamonds and rubies. "For a *real* princess!" he said.

The royal wedding was lavish and elegant, and a great deal of money and care was spent on the festivities. It seemed as if half the kingdom was in attendance, so curious was everyone to get a glimpse of Elaine. Certainly, the ceremonies were perfect for the most handsome prince in the land and the most beautiful, kind, and loving *real* princess.

The King, the Queen, and all the royal court were so happy that they sang and danced into the night and did not get to bed until well after dawn.

The Prince and Princess lived long and happily. In time, Andre and Elaine had several children, all of whom were girls, that is, *real* princesses, possessing all the beauties—and all the frailties—of their position.

As we all know, true royalty not only has trouble getting a good night's rest, but has delicate skin that bruises easily.

So it was decreed that the young princesses would sleep only on mattresses of the softest eiderdown— and that dried peas would be banished from the palace pantry!

Snow White

Once there was a lovely young princess whose skin was so pale that she was called Snow White. Her life would have been wonderful, but her wicked and vain stepmother, the Queen, treated her cruelly.

Daily, the Queen would look into her magic mirror and ask who the loveliest woman in the kingdom was. The mirror answered faithfully, "You may be cruel, you may be mean—but you are also the fairest, my Queen."

The years passed, and Snow White grew up. One day, the mirror gave a quite different response. "You are indeed cruel, you are indeed mean—and Snow White is now the fairest, my Queen." The vain Queen flew into a jealous rage and banished Snow White to the forest.

Deep in the woods and all alone, Snow White began to cry. She was hungry, tired, frightened, and lost. A friendly blue jay heard her sobs. Looking into the girl's heart (as all birds can do), he saw that she was kind and good and so decided to help her.

The jay fluttered softly around her head, then led her to a small cottage tucked into the side of a mountain.

Looking in the hut's window, Snow White saw a table set for seven, but the knives, forks, plates, cups, and napkins were exceedingly tiny. She was so hungry that she went in uninvited and helped herself to a little something from each plate.

$\mathcal{I}$n the next room, she found seven neat little beds all in a row. She was so tired that she stretched across all seven and fell soundly asleep.

Soon after, the seven dwarfs who lived in the cottage came home and were surprised to find their fair guest. They had spent the day mining gold and diamonds deep in the mountain. When they woke Snow White, she told them her sad story.

Looking into her heart (as all dwarfs can do), they saw that Snow White was kind and good, and they decided to help her.

"Stay here with us," the eldest advised. "We will keep you safe."

At the castle, the Queen was in a rage once more. Whenever she asked the mirror who was the prettiest, she received the reply, "You are wicked, you are vile, and you are a beauty rare. But Snow White, who is deep in the woods, is easily the most fair."

Furious, the Queen decided to kill Snow White. She dressed as a peddler, prepared a poison comb, and hurried off. The Queen raged through the forest like a storm, breaking young saplings and stomping wildflowers, until she came upon Snow White working in the garden outside the cottage.

With a sweet, sly smile, the Queen offered her the comb. Snow White—dear, innocent Snow White—took it gratefully, but as soon as it was in her hair, she fell into a deep sleep.

When the dwarfs returned from their day's work, they rushed to Snow White's side.

"The wicked Queen must have found her and done this," said the youngest dwarf sadly. He reached down to stroke her hair, and as he did he knocked the comb loose.

Snow White awoke at once and thanked him. She broke the poison comb into many small pieces.

When the Queen returned home, she quickly asked the mirror who was fairest. To her dismay, the mirror said, "Despite your truly evil plan, Snow White is still the fairest in the land." The fierce Queen shook with anger.

Carrying a basket of poisoned apples and disguised as a peasant woman, the Queen returned to the cottage the next day. Snow White was again working in the garden, and the jealous Queen offered her one of the apples.

"Why, thank you," said Snow White. "I am quite hungry, and the fruit does look delicious . . . ."

She raised the apple to her lips and took a small bite. Immediately, she fell to the ground, and the Queen hurried away, laughing wickedly.

Now that she was sure that Snow White was dead, the evil Queen rushed back to the castle. She stood before her magic mirror and once again asked, "Mirror, mirror on the wall, now who is the fairest one of all?"

The mirror replied, "Gone is the beauty of Snow White, and you are the fairest in my sight." There seemed a hint of sadness in the mirror's voice as it spoke these fateful words.

The Queen, however, did not notice. The mirror had told her exactly what she wanted to hear. And so, far from showing any sadness, the Queen laughed triumphantly at her good fortune.

The dwarfs returned home that evening to find Snow White lying on the ground. With tears in their eyes, they laid her still body on a soft bed of rose petals and moss and sat down to watch over her.

In time, a young prince riding through the forest came upon the group. "What a strange sight," he said to himself.

The Prince halted his horse and let himself down. Kneeling next to the bed of rose petals so that he could see her face more clearly, the Prince was overwhelmed by Snow White's great beauty. Looking into her heart (as only a very few people can do), he saw that she was kind and good, and he fell instantly in love with her.

As the dwarfs looked on, the Prince raised Snow White's head, for he longed to be closer to her. He gazed lovingly on her face and stroked her cheek. As he did so, he jostled her, and the piece of apple fell from her mouth, causing Snow White to awaken.

First, she looked into the Prince's eyes and saw that he loved her. Then, she looked into the Prince's heart (as the dwarfs had taught her to do), and Snow White could see that he was not only a loving man, but a kind and good one.

She felt love and gratitude stir in her heart, for the Prince had saved her from a cruel fate, waking her as if from the dead.

The Prince was astonished. It was several minutes before he could speak. But when he finally found his tongue, he came quickly to the point. "I do not know your name, maiden, but will you marry me even so?" he begged.

"My name is Snow White," replied the girl, looking first at the Prince, then at the dwarfs gathered around her. All of them nodded vigorously, as if urging her to say yes. (They had looked into the hearts of the Prince and Snow White and saw that the two were meant for each other.) "And I will gladly marry you!" Snow White added with a warm smile.

The two set a wedding date a few days later. Unable to contain themselves, the dwarfs danced and rejoiced.

Alas, there was little happiness at the palace, for a few days later when the Queen asked her mirror who was now the fairest in the land, the silvery image intoned, "Oh, Queen, you are a beauty rare, but the bride Snow White will always be more fair."

The Queen once more flew into a rage, cursing the day she had first set eyes on Snow White. At that, a small smile crept across the face in the mirror.

The Steadfast Tin Soldier

Once there were twenty-five tin soldiers in a wooden box. Each was brave. Each was handsome and wore a smart blue uniform. But one soldier, Will, had only one leg. He had been made last, and the toymaker had run out of tin.

But Will stood just as straight on his one leg as the others did on two, and he was just as brave and handsome.

The soldiers were given to a boy on his birthday. He opened the box and stood them up in a straight row on the table. Will looked around and saw that he was in a nursery. There were many other toys in the room and a colorful box on the floor. On the far side of the table, he saw a castle made of paper. In the doorway of the castle stood a beautiful paper maiden. Will fell in love with her at once.

The paper maiden, whose name was Alyssa, was a dancer. One arm was raised above her head, and one foot was lifted so high behind her that Will thought she had only one leg, just like him. She wore a short dress made of sky blue gauze with a blue ribbon on one sleeve.

"She would make a perfect wife for me," thought Will. He gazed and gazed at the paper maid, unable to take his eyes off her.

Evening came, and the boy put all the soldiers except Will back in the box. When it grew dark, the toys began to play. The tin soldier stood stiffly at attention and watched Alyssa. She stood still and looked at him out of the corner of her eye.

Suddenly, the lid flew off the colorful box and landed on the floor. Out popped an ugly, evil goblin. The goblin shrieked at the soldier, "Stop staring at the paper dancer!" But Will kept his eyes on her. "You'll pay for this!" screamed the goblin.

The next morning the boy took the soldier and stood him on the windowsill. Suddenly, a gust of wind blew—probably caused by the goblin. Will fell out the window, and his hat stuck in the dirt between stones in the street below.

Soon, it began to rain. The rain came down so hard and fast that water ran in torrents down the street. Will bravely waited for the downpour to end. When it was over, two boys found the toy soldier. They made a paper boat, put Will in it, and floated him down a canal.

The canal emptied into a dark tunnel. The waters were so swift that the paper boat whirled and tipped dangerously, but the tin soldier held fast and was very brave. How he wished the beautiful Alyssa could be here with him! Then he would have been happy.

A big rat that lived in the tunnel loomed up beside the boat.

"Where is your pass?" the rat demanded. "Give me your pass at once."

The tin soldier remained still and steady. The rat swam fast after the boat, shrieking and slapping the water. But the boat whirled too fast in the current.

Soon the rat was left behind. Will could hear the sound of the rat's voice fading as the boat whirled on. He let out a great sigh of relief.

Will wondered what the goblin had in store for him next and if he would ever see Alyssa again. The current grew stronger and stronger, pulling the boat along faster and faster. Just as Will began to see daylight at the end of the tunnel, he heard a terrible roar and splashing. Will's boat was heading straight for a waterfall.

He knew the poor, soggy boat could never survive a waterfall, but there was no stopping the current. He pulled himself up and stood more bravely then ever on his one leg.

Once the soggy paper boat was caught in the rushing waterfall, it quickly filled with water and sank.

"This must certainly be my end," thought the tin soldier as he plunged swiftly down into the whirlpool. "I will never again see the beautiful Alyssa, nor will I know how wonderful it would have been to watch her dance for me."

'Round and 'round he whirled. His shiny blue uniform caught the eye of a large fish swimming by. The fish stopped, looked Will over from head to toe, and then swallowed him in one gulp.

*I*t was much darker in the fish than in the tunnel, but Will held himself as straight as he could. The fish seemed to dash around frantically for a time and then lay quiet.

After a long time there was a flash like lightning and Will saw daylight again. The fish had been caught on someone's hook. Now it was in a kitchen, and the cook was preparing it for dinner.

"My goodness! Look at this old tin soldier inside my fish!" exclaimed the cook. She pulled Will out, then wiped him off and brought him to the nursery.

Will looked around and saw the box where his brothers were kept, the goblin's box on the floor, and the paper castle. His tin heart beat faster when he realized that he was home. The boy came into the nursery and looked at the tin soldier.

"Where have you been?" the boy asked in an accusing tone. "You're damp, and you smell like a fish."

Suddenly, he opened the window and threw Will into the flower garden below. Will lay among the petunias and felt sad, but he stayed straight and brave.

"The evil goblin must be very glad!" he thought.

Just then a gentle wind blew over him, whispering softly. It blew through the house, caught up Alyssa, and blew her straight out the open window into the garden.

With a graceful little flutter, the paper dancer landed next to Will among the petunias.

They looked at each other with beating hearts and adoring eyes. Then they slid very close together.

"Will you stay with me and be my wife?" Will asked.

"Yes, forever and ever!" she whispered.

And that is just what she did. They were married soon after beneath the leaves of a low-growing plant, and the flowers danced over them, hiding them from all the world. The wind whispered softly, rustling the trees like music.

Days and nights passed. The winds blew, and rain and snow fell on the tin soldier and his bride, but the sun shone on them and dried them off. Sometimes a cat or a dog or a bird, prowling through the flowers and bushes, would come upon Will and Alyssa. None ever made trouble, however, since no one knew what to make of the tin soldier and his paper doll.

And so, Will and Alyssa were happy, for, aside from an occasional visitor, there was no evil goblin, no fat rat, no hungry fish to torment them.

Sometimes, when the full moon shone through the branches above and the air was balmy and warm, the graceful Alyssa would dance for her husband, pirouetting in the gentle night breezes and dancing to music made by the wind in the trees.

She always remained true to Will, as did the Steadfast Tin Soldier to her.

Thumbelina

Once upon a time, a childless woman wanted a little girl very much—so much so that she set aside her fears and begged the help of a witch.

"A *little* girl you shall have, dearie!" the witch cackled. She gave the woman a seed to plant, and lo and behold, a single flower soon shot up. When the sky blue flower opened, out popped the loveliest—and littlest—blonde-haired girl, no bigger than the woman's thumb!

She was named Thumbelina and was given many luxuries, such as a walnut-shell cradle with a rose-petal blanket and a thimble of nectar to drink morning, noon, and evening.

One night, a wart-faced toad spied her through the window. "What a delightful bride she'll make for my son!" croaked the mother toad.

The old toad seized the cradle with the sleeping girl in it and hopped off to a nearby stream.

"Ribbitt! Chuggarrumpff!" croaked her son.

"Quiet," the mother shushed as she set the cradle on a lily pad, "or you'll wake her!"

At daybreak, Thumbelina stretched, yawned—and saw that something was dreadfully wrong. The mother toad introduced her son to Thumbelina. "I just know you two will be happy together!" the elder toad croaked. The two toads hopped away to build a new home for the couple, and Thumbelina wept.

A school of pike heard her sobs and decided to help. They bit through the stalk of her lily pad, and Thumbelina drifted away on the water.

As Thumbelina floated downstream, a black-winged beetle flying overhead noticed her. "What a remarkable creature," he thought. "I'll bring her home with me."

He swooped down and snatched her off to a dim forest. His fellow beetles gathered around and looked at Thumbelina carefully.

"Ugh! Look at all that long, shiny hair," said one.

"And she has only two legs!" said another. The beetles decided that they had no use for such an unattractive thing, and they sent her away, even though the beetle who brought her hoped she could stay. Thumbelina was left to wander alone in the forest as the cold winter winds began to blow.

As she wandered, shivering and hungry, Thumbelina stumbled over a small hole in the ground.

"Who's there?" demanded a squeaky voice. But Thumbelina's lips were too frozen to move.

"Dear, dear," said a field mouse as she poked her nose out of the hole. "Come inside before you catch your death!" The mouse could be quite friendly when she wanted something, and she offered Thumbelina a home for the winter.

"But you must keep house and tell stories at teatime," insisted the mouse, "and do the same for my neighbor. He's a wealthy mole who, by the way, is looking for a wife—"

At that instant, a furry head with spectacles poked its pink nose through the entrance.

"Why, speak of the devil!" shrieked the mouse. "Mole, allow me to present Thumbelina."

"Charmed, I'm sure," mumbled the nearsighted mole as he bowed low. "Mouse, you simply must see how the new tunnel is coming along."

The mole took the mouse and Thumbelina down a dark passageway that he had been digging between their burrows. On the way, the three passed the frozen body of a swallow.

"Never mind him, Thumbelina," said the mouse.

"Be glad you have arms instead of wings," muttered the mole, "and more sense than to let yourself freeze to death."

That night, Thumbelina went back to where the bird lay. Listening at his breast, she heard the faintest heartbeat, so she covered him with a grass blanket and put her arms around him. After a while, the bird opened his eyes.

"Where am I?" chirped the swallow, coming to his senses. "You've saved me! However can I thank you?"

Thumbelina promised to nurse the swallow until he was strong enough to fly.

Meanwhile, the mouse, who wanted a maid, and the mole, who wanted a wife *and* a maid, agreed that Thumbelina was just what they were looking for. They decided that when summer came, Thumbelina and the mole would be married.

The day came for the swallow to depart. He asked Thumbelina to go with him, but she thought it would be unkind to leave after the mouse had been so nice to her. The swallow sadly twittered good-bye and flew away.

Down below, the mouse called for yet another teatime story, and when Thumbelina returned, the mouse told her the mole had asked for her hand in marriage.

Thumbelina refused to marry the mole, but the mouse insisted that she must. Soon, the wedding day arrived, and so did the mole, wearing a frock coat and carrying two plain gold bands.

Poor Thumbelina ran above ground. "Oh, why didn't I fly away when I had the chance?" she cried.

Suddenly, a winged shadow passed overhead. "Better late than never!" called the swallow. "Will you come with me now?"

Thumbelina joyfully climbed on his back, and the two flew south to a magical land of clear waters, powdery beaches, and flowers that blossomed all through the year.

The swallow lowered Thumbelina onto a daisy and flew away. The girl looked right and left—and noticed a handsome young man perched on a nearby flower. He had transparent wings and a gold crown, and best of all he was just about Thumbelina's size. Their eyes met, and they fell in love instantly.

"I am King of the Daisies," said the young man, gesturing toward little winged lords and ladies who peeked from behind flower petals. "I have thousands of subjects, but none like you! Be my queen!" he begged as he kissed Thumbelina's hand.

"I will gladly be your wife," Thumbelina replied.

The King's subjects flew to Thumbelina and presented her with a pair of gossamer wings that fit her perfectly.

The couple then soared up into the cloudless blue sky where, flying in ever-widening circles, the loyal swallow waited patiently.

The Frog Prince

Once there was a young princess named Jade who decided to go for a walk in the forest. She brought along her kitten, Minerva, and her favorite toy, a small golden ball. When she came to a beautiful, cool spring, she sat down to rest. While Minerva chased butterflies, Jade tossed her ball and caught it again.

After a time, she tossed it too hard, and the ball fell into the spring. The Princess peered into it, but the water was too deep. She could not see her golden ball.

"Oh, oh!" she cried. "I would give all my jewels and beautiful clothes if only I could have my golden ball back."

While she was sobbing by the side of the spring, an ugly green frog stuck his head out of the water.

"What's wrong?" he asked. "Why are you crying?"

"You can't help," she said. "You're only an ugly frog."

But the frog told her he could get her ball. All he wanted in return was to live with her, to eat from her plate, and to sleep in her bed. Now this seemed very strange, but Jade thought the frog would never come to the palace. So she agreed to do as the frog wished.

The frog swam to the bottom of the spring, brought up the golden ball in his mouth, and dropped it at her feet.

Jade was so happy that she grabbed her golden ball and ran home with Minerva, forgetting all about the frog. After all, how could a frog leave its home in the spring?

"Wait!" called the frog after her, but Jade ran on.

The next day, just as the royal family sat down to dinner, there was a knock at the door. The princess herself answered it. To her amazement, there sat the frog. He began to sing:

"Princess, my princess, I pray I'm not late.
I'll sleep in your bed and I'll eat from your plate."

The Princess was so frightened to see him there that she slammed the door and went back to the table.

"Who was there?" asked the King.

"What a strange little song!" remarked the Queen.

When Jade told them the story, the King shook his head and said, "If you gave your word, you must keep it, Jade." Her mother agreed, so Jade went to the door and let the frog in. He came tap, tap, splash, splash across the marble floor. Then he gave a leap and was sitting beside Jade at the table.

"Move your plate closer so that I may eat from it," he begged, and Jade did. When they were finished, he and Minerva followed her up the marble steps to her bedroom.

Jade felt sure she could not sleep a wink with that frog in her bed. But he rolled himself in the edge of the covers and stayed quite out of her way, so all three slept soundly.

When morning came, the frog gave a little bow, hopped down the stairs, and went off toward the forest. Jade hugged Minerva close and breathed a sigh.

"That's the end of him," she told Minerva.

But the next evening, just as the royal family sat down to dinner, there was a knock at the door.

Jade opened it, and there was the ugly green frog as before, singing his song again. Before she could say, "Go away!" he had tap, tapped, splash, splashed across the floor and leaped onto her chair as before. Minerva hissed and arched her back, but Jade moved her plate closer to the frog.

When they were finished, he hopped up the marble stairs behind her and leaped onto her bed. This night, Jade didn't mind the frog so much. After all, he was such a polite frog—and he sang so very nicely.

The next morning, the frog returned to the forest. On the third night he was back again.

Jade was starting to wonder if the frog was going to make his home with her. She thought it might not be so very bad. He seemed kind and might make a good friend. Even Minerva didn't mind as much.

The frog ate from her plate and climbed into her bed as usual the third night. But before he fell asleep, he sang another song:

"You have kept your word and now at sunrise,
You will be rewarded with a surprise."

The princess wondered about it for a long time before she fell asleep. Whatever could the frog mean?

When Jade awoke at sunrise she was astonished to see the most handsome prince she could ever have imagined. He was standing by her bed gazing at her. The frog was gone. The prince's name was Roland. He told her he had long ago been enchanted by a wicked fairy. The fairy had changed him into a frog and thrown him into the forest spring.

"You will remain as a frog," she had said, "until some princess lets you eat from her plate and sleep in her bed for three nights."

"And so you did!" Prince Roland said. "Come with me to my father's kingdom and be my wife. I will love you as long as I live!"

Jade could hardly believe what was happening.

"Yes," she said. "I will marry you!"

They ran downstairs to tell the wonderful news to the King and Queen. Jade's parents were amazed to see a strange prince in their house. But Roland explained about the enchantment and the fairy.

"And then this morning, there he was, standing by my bed!" Jade exclaimed. "And I knew I wanted to marry him. Even when he was still a frog, I had started to care for him. True kindness and goodness cannot be disguised by an ugly appearance."

$\mathcal{J}$ade's father gave his blessing to the young couple and his thanks to Prince Roland.

"You have taught my daughter Jade not only the meaning of patience, but the importance of being true to one's word," said the King.

Soon afterward, Princess Jade and Prince Roland were married in a beautiful palace ceremony. Nearly everyone from around the kingdom came to see the Prince, miraculously transformed from a frog to a handsome young man because of Jade's good deed.

Then, with a tearful farewell, the couple departed for Roland's native country. There, his parents, the King and Queen of that land, made them welcome.

From that day forward, Jade was careful how she treated the small animals of the forest, for she was never exactly sure which one was bewitched and which one was not!

Pinocchio

Long ago, a poor old craftsman named Geppetto spent his days creating splendid wooden dolls and puppets. The old man's greatest joy—besides his dog, Trooper—was the shining eyes and excited laughter of the children who played with his toys. He was happy with work and with life, but he did have one secret wish: that someday he would be father to a real boy.

A blue-winged fairy wanted to reward Geppetto for his good heart. She waved her magic wand as he carved a figure from a piece of fresh, soft pine wood. The little puppet seemed to come alive and wiggle in his hands.

"You are the finest puppet I have ever made," Geppetto marveled when he finished. "I will call you Pinocchio. Now, hold still so I can paint you, dear boy!"

As soon as the old carver finished, Pinocchio jumped up and scampered around the room. Eager to see the whole world, the careless little puppet ran out the door and into the village square. Such a wonderful place—shops, vendors of fruit, bread, and sausages! He darted through the crowd, looking at every stall and in every window.

Geppetto and Trooper ran after Pinocchio, thinking he might get into mischief. To be sure, he did. Looking up and not ahead, Pinocchio did not see a cart piled high with wheels of cheese. With a bump and a crash, the puppet and the cheese met.

Pinocchio ran—and so did the town constable. The policeman grabbed Pinocchio by the collar, saying, "This one needs to be in school, not in trouble!"

Geppetto knew that Pinocchio should be in school. The old carver sold his only coat to buy Pinocchio a schoolbook. He gave it to him, saying, "Pinocchio, to be like a real boy, you must go to school. Now, be on your way, and take Trooper with you. He'll guide you."

Pinocchio started off to school, with Trooper following close behind. At the corner, Pinocchio heard the music of the local puppet theater and stopped to watch the show. Now, Trooper knew that Pinocchio shouldn't stay, so he began growling and tugging at the puppet's sleeve. "Trooper, leave me be! I want to watch." But Trooper just growled louder.

The noise interrupted the show, and Signore Grumbolo, the puppet master, became very angry. He shouted at Pinocchio and Trooper and chased them away.

Pinocchio and Trooper went on their way. At the next turn, they met a sly fox. When the fox heard that Pinocchio was on his way to school, he shook his head and laughed.

"Oh no, no, no, my friend! That is not for you. Real boys don't want school. They want to sail across the Truant Sea to Runaway Island, where they have fun and play all day! I could sell you a ticket, if you like."

Trooper didn't care for the fox or his ideas, and he tried to let Pinocchio know. But some puppets just won't listen. Quicker than a wink, Pinocchio sold his schoolbook for a ticket to Runaway Island. He was going to be a real boy and have fun.

As the fox ran off, the blue-winged fairy appeared. "Pinocchio, why aren't you going to school?" she asked.

"Oh, but I am! I was just . . . I was just helping that fellow find his way to town." And with that big lie, Pinocchio's nose began to grow longer and longer until a butterfly flew down and perched on it.

Pinocchio began to cry. He promised to be a good boy and go straight to school. The fairy forgave him and, with a sweep of her wand, he got his old nose back.

When Pinocchio arrived at school, he met Wickley, a boy who was leaving for Runaway Island. Not thinking about Geppetto or the blue-winged fairy and not listening to Trooper, Pinocchio went along.

At first, Runaway Island seemed wonderful: It was all carnivals and sweets and bicycles and no one telling you what to do. Pinocchio and Wickley played all day. Trooper stayed close by, but would have nothing to do with the fun.

They stopped by a lake to rest, and as Pinocchio dipped his hand into the water for a drink, he saw his reflection. Heavens! He had grown long ears and a tail like a donkey. He turned to Wickley and saw that it was happening to him, too, and to all the other boys on the island. Pinocchio cried out, "Oh, help! Somebody help me!"

Once again, the blue-winged fairy appeared. "Foolish puppet," she said, wagging her finger at him. "Lose those donkey ways and go find your poor father, who weeps for you!"

With a wave of her wand, the fairy made the donkey ears and tail disappear. She sent Pinocchio down to the seashore, where he could see Geppetto far out to sea in a small boat. As any father would do, the old man was searching tirelessly for his lost son.

Pinocchio called out to him, and the water began to churn and foam terribly. From the depths of the sea, a huge wave rolled up, and on that wave rode a giant dogfish that swallowed up Geppetto, boat and all.

Thinking only of his father, Pinocchio jumped into the water, swam out to the dogfish, and jumped down his throat without even blinking.

Deep in the belly of the fish, Pinocchio and Geppetto hugged each other and danced with joy. They were so happy to be together. But how to get out?

Geppetto thought and thought, but he could not come up with a plan. As they sat and schemed, they heard an enormous rumbling noise that seemed to come from everywhere. "Snoring!" cried Pinocchio. "The fish is asleep! Come on, Father, when he opens his mouth to snore, we'll slide down his tongue and slip out between his teeth!"

And that's exactly what happened. In a moment, father and son were free again.

But they were still far from shore, and Geppetto was a poor swimmer. The little puppet grabbed hold of the old man and pulled him ashore.

Geppetto awoke with the waves gently lapping at his feet. At his side stood the watchful Trooper, softly barking. And next to Geppetto sat, of all things, a little boy—made not of soft pine, but of flesh, blood, and bone!

And so it was that Pinocchio had finally learned the simplest and yet most important lesson: that being a real person means nothing more—but nothing less— than loving and caring for others.

The Emperor's New Clothes

Many years ago, there was an emperor named Pardonius. He lived in a splendid palace and loved clothes—to distraction. He loved them so much that he had his tailors make him a new outfit every day. He was especially fond of colors, and his greatest delight was mixing gorgeous reds, purples, blues, and yellows.

Most other kings or emperors were busy ruling their lands. Pardonius, however, was always in his dressing rooms or parading in the palace gardens to show off his finery.

Many people came to visit the city where Pardonius ruled, and life there was full of celebration.

One day, two thieves who were extremely clever men came to town. The thieves let it be known that they were famous weavers.

"We can weave fine cloth for you," they told Pardonius, who invited them to court out of curiosity. "It will be worthy of your empire. The threads of this cloth are woven so finely that only very intelligent people can see it. People who are either fools or unfit for the office they hold cannot see it at all!"

The Emperor thought this would be an excellent way to find out who at court was not carrying out his duties. He hired the two thieves at once.

Pardonius gave the thieves a large sum of money. He ordered a supply of the most expensive silk and linen thread for them to weave.

The weavers set up large looms and pretended to weave, but their shuttles were empty. All the expensive thread and the money went straight into their pockets.

Day and night they worked, climbing up ladders to reach the tops of the looms and moving their hands in the air, pretending to weave. "See," they explained, "we are the only weavers in the land who can make such cloth!" When no one was around to see them, they rested and laughed heartily because they were becoming rich.

Pardonius wanted to see the new cloth, but he was a little afraid to pay the weavers a visit.

"What if I cannot see it?" he wondered. "It might mean I am unfit to be emperor."

So he asked his faithful old minister, Percival, to inspect the work for him. Percival went into the weaving room. The thieves were working away at their empty looms.

"Oh, my goodness!" thought the minister. "I can't see a thing!" But Percival liked his job at the palace, so he pretended to see the wondrous cloth.

"How do you like it, sir?" asked the thieves. "Aren't the colors superb? Isn't the pattern marvelous?"

"Yes, indeed!" the old minister answered, and he strained hard to see the cloth. He went back and told the Emperor how wonderful it was.

A little later, Pardonius was again curious about how the work was progressing. This time he sent another faithful official, Gaylord, to see the cloth. As had happened with Percival, Gaylord could see nothing, but he pretended he could see the nonexistent cloth. He reported to the Emperor how wonderful it was.

$\mathfrak{F}$inally, Pardonius could wait no longer. He called the thieves to his court. "You are taking a long time," he observed.

"Ah, yes," said one. "It takes time and special skill to make such fine cloth."

"I shall come see it," Pardonius said.

He summoned ten of his officials, Percival and Gaylord among them. They went into the weaving room where the crafty imposters were seemingly hard at work. "It is magnificent!" the officials said. "See, your Majesty! What a design!"

But the Emperor could see nothing. He moaned inwardly, thinking, "I must not be fit to rule my own kingdom!" Aloud, he said, "The colors are simply gorgeous!" And everyone agreed!

The thieves asked for more money and more fine thread to finish the job, and Pardonius ordered it. He even ordered two badges of knighthood for the weavers to wear on their jackets.

The Great Annual Procession was soon to take place in the city. Pardonius asked the two imposters to make him a royal suit from the cloth at once. Many candles burned down as the two worked through the night, cutting and measuring the empty air. Their needles clicked and clacked, but had no thread in them.

Just before the great procession, they announced, "The Emperor's new clothes are finished!"

The thieves called Pardonius into their room and helped him take off all his clothes. Then they pretended to fit him, one piece at a time, in the marvelous new clothes. They pretended to fasten something around his waist and to put a sash over his shoulder. They raised their arms as though lifting a heavy train, which they handed to the Emperor's pages to carry.

The thieves turned Pardonius round and round in front of the mirror and told him he looked magnificent. All in attendance agreed wholeheartedly.

The procession began. People lined both sides of the street and hung out their windows to see the Emperor's new clothes.

No one could see the clothes, of course, because there were no clothes to see. But each person was afraid to be thought a fool, so everyone pretended to see the royal robes. Many "Oh's" and "Ah's!" went up from the crowd.

Children came to see the Emperor, too. One clever boy, his eyes wide with amusement, called out, "The Emperor has no clothes on at all!"

Suddenly, everyone realized the truth. The magical cloth was only air. Pardonius knew it was true, too, but he held himself stiffly and finished the procession. By the time he returned to the palace, the thieves were far away with the Emperor's money.

"I have been a silly old fool!" wept Pardonius. "My subjects now know what a poor ruler I have been. How can they ever forgive my vanity, my blindness? I have made myself look ridiculous. However will I regain their respect?"

The Emperor resolved, then and there, to become a better man. No longer would he let his passion for new clothes blind him to his real duty, leading and serving his people. The next day, he summoned the boy to court.

"You saw what no one else would admit to seeing," said Pardonius. "From now on, you shall live in the palace with me and warn me when I am about to do something foolish!"

There were many times when the Emperor was on the verge of doing something stupid or shameful—like ordering a dozen pairs of new boots when he already had a closetful, or commissioning a new silver service when solid-gold forks and knives and spoons still lay untouched in their packing crates. The boy would always tug on the Emperor's sleeve and whisper in his ear.

And so it was that Pardonius, with the boy's help, came to be known as the wisest of emperors.

The Little Mermaid

In the darkest, deepest part of the ocean lived the old Sea King, his six mermaid daughters, and the girls' grandmother. The Sea King had a long grizzled beard, and he ruled the ocean creatures with wisdom and kindness.

The youngest of the daughters, Princess Melody, had blue eyes, long blonde hair, and a sweet voice. All who heard it could not help but stop what they were doing and listen. No one could resist Melody's singing.

Being a mermaid, Melody had a fishtail instead of legs. It helped her swim underwater and play with her dolphin friend.

Grandmother told many stories to the young mermaids as they laughed and combed their long hair. The mermaids had their favorite tales, and they made Grandmother tell them over and over again. Some of the best stories were about strange creatures, called human beings, who lived above the water and moved about on legs.

It was the custom that a mermaid be allowed to swim to the surface on her sixteenth birthday to see these strange beings. Melody could hardly wait!

On that day, Grandmother took Melody aside to give her advice: "Today is a special day for you. You may swim up to see the humans, but you may not speak to them, and you must return at once." Melody darted to the surface as quickly as she could fan her fishtail.

When Melody reached the ocean's waves, she saw a sailing ship anchored in the distance. She swam over and was amazed to see so many strange creatures—two-legged ones—strolling and dancing on deck.

One of the creatures was a tall, handsome prince. She could tell he was a prince because he had a crown on his head, just as she did. Melody sighed, "Oh, I think I am in love with this wonderful being."

Just then, a bolt of lightning flashed, the sky turned black, and the waves rose up. The storm lifted the ship high on the waves, then snapped it in two. The Prince was hit on the head by the ship's mast and knocked overboard. He was too dazed to swim and began to sink beneath the sea.

Melody's crown slipped off as she rushed to catch the Prince, but her dolphin friend caught it in his mouth. She flipped her tail and carried the Prince to the nearest shore. His eyes were closed, so he did not see who had saved him. But he did hear her sing to him as she swam. Melody left the Prince on the shore and swam back out to sea.

She waited to see who would come to help the Prince. Before long, some children found him lying on the sand. They called their mother, who recognized him. She hurried to the palace to spread the news that the Prince was alive. Everyone at court thought that he had died in the storm.

With tears in her eyes, Melody swam back to her sisters. "Oh, how I want to be like human creatures," she sobbed.

"I can't forget my handsome Prince. I must have legs so I can be with him," Melody wept to her grandmother. Grandmother told Melody that only a magic spell, chanted by the Sea Witch, could help her.

So Melody went to see the Sea Witch in her cavern guarded by sea dragons. The Sea Witch agreed to help. She would give the mermaid human legs, but Melody would have to give the Sea Witch her magnificent voice in exchange. Melody was unhappy, but she agreed to make the trade.

Handing Melody a silver cup with a magic drink, the Sea Witch said, "Fishtail, fishtail, split in two. Give legs to this mermaid sweet and true." Melody felt her head spin as she sang good-bye.

When Melody opened her eyes, she was sitting on a sandy beach, and her tail had been replaced with two long, smooth human legs. She realized that this was the place where she had left the Prince.

The Prince happened to be strolling along the shore. He saw the girl and approached her. "Who are you? Where do you come from?" he inquired.

Melody tried to answer, but she had no voice. All she could do was motion with her hands.

"Never mind," said the Prince. "My name is Kyle. You can come back to the palace, and I will take care of you." He brought her to his home and was kind to her. Still, he longed to meet the lady with the beautiful voice who had rescued him.

Melody and Prince Kyle saw each other every day. They would take long walks on the beach and sometimes go sailing on the royal boat. Melody loved to just sit and look at her Prince.

Since she had lost her beautiful voice, Melody could neither speak nor sing. She learned to use gestures to tell Prince Kyle what she wanted to say. The Prince was enchanted watching Melody "speak" with her graceful hands.

The days and nights were filled with laughter, and Prince Kyle made sure that all in the palace treated Melody with kindness, for she was his best friend.

Melody was happy with her new legs and her newfound friend, but the Sea Witch was unhappy with her new voice.

The crystal ball she used to plan her magic spells would not respond to her commands, no matter how fierce she tried to sound. The fish and other creatures of the sea no longer feared her—now that her voice was sweet and soothing, they swam in and around her cave, playing tag with the sea dragon guards.

Nobody took the Sea Witch seriously anymore. Her sweet and beautiful voice canceled the spells that she tried to cast.

"This cannot go on," she finally decreed. "I must get my own fearsome voice back!"

One morning, Melody and Prince Kyle were sailing on the royal boat. Melody heard the Sea Witch singing, "Melody, Melody, I haven't much choice: You may keep your new legs, but give back my voice."

Melody opened her mouth and, to everyone's surprise, out poured a beautiful, sweet song. The prince quickly recognized the voice of the young woman who had saved him. He asked her to marry him that very day.

The wedding was held on the deck of the ship as the Sea King, Grandmother, Melody's sisters, and all her other sea friends looked on. Then the ship sailed over the horizon into the setting sun, bound for exotic lands.

The Jungle Book

Father Wolf woke from his nap in the cave and watched Mother Wolf nuzzling their four cubs. The sound of an angry, snarling tiger came on the wind. "It is Shere Khan," said Father Wolf. "Listen, he hunts Man tonight."

"Must he eat Man on our grounds?" complained Mother Wolf. It was against the Jungle Law, after all. They could hear the tiger charge, then a high shriek fading into the jungle told them that the prey had escaped. The bushes rustled outside the cave, and Father Wolf went out to see what had made the sound.

"A Man-cub," he gasped. "Look!"

Mother Wolf saw a baby, just old enough to begin walking, at the cave's mouth.

$\mathcal{F}$ather Wolf caught him in his powerful jaws and gently laid him on the dirt floor. The boy crawled over to the cubs, and soon they were all playing together.

"He is so little," Mother Wolf said softly. "See, he is not afraid! I would like to keep him. I will call him Mowgli, little frog, because he has no fur."

Suddenly the great head of Shere Khan thrust itself into the cave. "The Man-cub!" roared the tiger. "He is mine! Give him to me!"

"We wolves are a free people," snarled Father Wolf. "We will keep him."

"And raise him with our own cubs," added Mother Wolf. "Go away!"

"What will the Wolf Pack say?" asked the sly Shere Khan, but the wolves were silent.

After the tiger left, Mother Wolf wondered what the pack *would* say, but for now the baby tumbled and played with her own cubs. He ate and slept with them and kept warm against Mother Wolf's coat.

When the cubs and Mowgli were old enough to run a little, Father Wolf took them to a hilltop for the Council of the Pack. Their leader was Akela, a strong and cunning brown wolf. He called each of the new cubs to be examined by the pack. Mowgli sat in the center when it was his turn, examining his fingers and toes.

Suddenly, a roar came from beyond the rocks. The wolves heard the voice of Shere Khan crying, "Give me the Man-cub! He is mine!"

"We, the Free People, will decide," Akela growled in retort. Turning to the pack, he asked, "Who speaks for the Man-cub?" It was a law of the jungle that two pack members, not parents, must speak for a cub if there was a dispute.

"I will speak!" said Baloo, a brown bear who was allowed in the pack because he taught the wolf cubs the Jungle Law. "There is no harm in a Man-cub. Let him run with the pack. I will teach him what he needs to know."

"Our teacher of young cubs has spoken," said Akela. "Is there another?"

A black shadow dropped into the circle. It was the coal-black panther Bagheera.

"I have no right to be in your meeting," purred Bagheera, "but I know a young cub can be bought for the pack. I will give you a freshly killed bull if you accept the Man-cub." Bagheera was wise and kind and did not want to see Mowgli cast into the jungle alone.

Voices rose, then one shouted, "Let us accept him! He'll never survive the scorching sun and winter rains."

"Men and their cubs are wise," said Akela. "He may help us in time." So Mowgli became one of the Wolf Pack, and Shere Khan could be heard roaring angrily into the night.

Mowgli was happy living among the wolves. Father Wolf and Baloo taught him the secrets of the jungle.

When Mowgli was not busy learning, he sat in the sun and ate or slept. When the day was too hot, he swam in forest pools. Baloo showed him where to find honey and nuts. Bagheera taught him to hide in the deep shadows of the jungle.

Sometimes Mowgli would pick thorns from the pads of his friends' paws or burrs from their long coats. Sometimes he went down the hillside to look at the mud huts of the village. He watched the villagers' children, who looked more like him than the wolves did. He wondered what it would be like to play with them.

Mowgli grew and grew. He was strong and happy, but sometimes he was unsure whether he was wolf or human.

One day, Bagheera and Mowgli were eating berries in the jungle when the panther said to him, "You know, Shere Khan is your enemy, and now you may have more dangerous ones."

He told Mowgli how Akela had grown old and weak. This very day he had missed a young buck in their hunt. Now the pack was ready to choose a stronger leader in Akela's place.

"Shere Khan has taught some of the young wolves that the Man-cub does not belong in the pack," said Bagheera. "I fear for you. Go down to the village and take some of the Red Flower. It will protect you."

That night, Mowgli crept into the village and watched a small boy tending a pot of burning red coals beside his hut. When the boy fell asleep, Mowgli took the pot and ran back into the jungle. There Mowgli fed twigs and dry bark into the pot as he had seen the boy do. He thrust a long branch into the Red Flower and watched one end burn.

All that day, Mowgli sat in the cave tending his fire pot. When evening came, he was called to the council on the hilltop. The pack had gathered, but Akela was sitting off to one side.

"A new leader!" they cried, one after the other. "Akela is too old, too weak!"

"The Man-cub!" roared Shere Khan from the rocks above. "Give him to me!"

The wolves rushed at Mowgli, shrieking, "Yes! Yes! Let us deliver him up so that Shere Khan may devour him!"

But Mowgli was too quick for them. He grabbed the fire pot and swung the Red Flower in a wide circle. Some of the burning coals flew out and set tufts of grass ablaze, frightening the wolves. Then, to strike real fear in their hearts, Mowgli dipped a branch into the pot. The end burst into flame. He swung it at Shere Khan and the pack, and they all fled in terror into the night.

Though he had saved himself and asserted his power, Mowgli knew that he had somehow crossed an invisible line between being an animal and being a human.

"I must go to the village now," Mowgli told Mother and Father Wolf. "I no longer belong in the jungle. It is in the village where, from now on, I must make my home among my fellow humans."

"We have loved you," they said. "Do not forget us." Mother Wolf nuzzled him one last time, tears coursing down her furry cheeks.

Mowgli wept long and bitterly, as little boys do when they must be parted from those they love. But he was firm in his decision to find a human family to live with.

And so, with nothing but the clothes he was wearing, Mowgli set out down the hillside, bound for the village and a new life among his own people. At the foot of the hill, he waved to Mother and Father Wolf.

Though he never saw his wolf parents again and never spoke of his early years, Mowgli did not forget the jungle he came from and the animals he first loved.

The Twelve Dancing Princesses

A long time ago, the King and Queen of a far-off land had twelve beautiful daughters. There were two sets of twins and two sets of triplets. The eldest and youngest had been born singly.

Every night, the princesses asked if they might go dancing. But the King always said no. Then he locked their bedroom door for good measure. Each morning, the princesses' shoes were tattered and full of holes, as if they had been dancing all night. Nobody could explain this, and the princesses would not tell.

The King sent an announcement to all the land, saying that anyone who could solve the mystery might choose one of the princesses as his wife. But if he did not find the answer in three nights, he would be imprisoned.

$\mathcal{M}$any young princes from distant kingdoms came to try. But they always fell asleep before they could solve the mystery. After the third night, they were thrown in prison.

One day, Michael, a poor lad from the country, came to try his luck. He had walked a very long time on the hard roads to reach the castle, and he was hungry and weary. Outside the gate, he came upon an old woman dressed in rags and carrying a wicker basket. She was stooped over, searching for something on the ground. Michael saw at once the coin she had dropped. He picked it up for her, and she thanked him humbly.

"I haven't eaten in two days. Could you spare me something from your market basket?" Michael asked.

The old woman smiled, showing her snaggle tooth, then reached into the basket and said, "Gladly, but I have something much better for you than food. You have helped me, and now I will help you. Here is a cloak to make you invisible. And above all, do not drink anything the princesses offer you."

Michael wondered how the old woman knew that he had come to solve the riddle of the princesses. But he took the cloak with thanks.

When he reached the castle, Michael asked the King's permission to try to solve the mystery. He was taken to a bedroom near the princesses. The eldest, Aurora, brought him a small cake and a cup of wine that, unknown to Michael, contained a sleeping potion. Michael ate the cake and, remembering the old woman's words, only pretended to drink the wine. Then he stretched out on his bed as if to sleep.

309

The princesses began to dress themselves in fancy clothes. They brushed their curls and decked themselves in jewels, laughing and singing all the while. But Alicia, the youngest, felt something was wrong.

"Wait! I fear there is trouble," she whispered.

"You only imagine it," said the doubting Aurora.

When they were ready, Aurora walked up to one of the beds and knocked three times on the headboard. At once it sank into the floor. A long passageway ending in a staircase opened up in the wall.

"Hurry!" called one of the triplets, and the princesses ran down the hall, one after the other.

Michael jumped up, put on the cloak that made him invisible, and hurried after them. In his haste, he stepped on the hem of Alicia's dress.

"Something clutched at my dress!" she cried.

"You just caught it on a nail," Aurora scoffed.

In a short while, they came to a forest. The leaves of the trees were made of silver and glowed in the moonlight. They rustled together, making a music of their own. Michael snapped off a silver leaf and slipped it into his pocket.

They passed through a second forest of trees with gold leaves, then through a third with diamond leaves.

At last they came to a castle whose highest towers were shrouded in fog. Twelve handsome princes waited outside and escorted the princesses into a large, beautiful ballroom. Everywhere there were lights and music. A long table was laden with wines, meats, poultry, breads, fruit, puddings, and cakes.

The princesses and princes ate and sipped their wine, then began to dance. Michael ate and drank, too, but they could not see him. Near morning, the princesses said good-bye to the princes and promised to come again the next night. They rushed back to their own castle, then up the stairway to their bedroom.

Michael had run ahead. Back in his room, he slipped off his cloak and jumped in bed.

"See," said Aurora, peeking in. "All is well!"

Michael had such a wonderful time in the enchanted castle that he decided to wait before he told the King. The second night, everything happened as before. This time, as they passed through the forest of gold leaves, Michael snapped one off and put it in his pocket.

On the third night, Michael decided to follow the princesses one last time. This night, when they passed through the forest of trees with diamond leaves, he snapped one off to put in his pocket. It make a cracking sound.

"What was that?" asked Alicia, so alarmed that she trembled.

But Aurora reassured her, saying, "It is nothing. You only imagined it!"

The princesses danced until dawn, and their shoes were full of holes again. Just before they left, Michael slipped one of the golden wine goblets into his pocket.

The next morning, the King summoned Michael to his court. Michael took the silver, gold, and diamond leaves and gold goblet to set before the King.

"Do you know where my daughters dance their shoes away?" asked the King.

Michael told him about the enchanted castle and the twelve dancing princes. The King called for the princesses to come to him.

"Does this young man tell the truth?" the King asked his daughters. The princesses saw the leaves and the goblet and knew they could not deny it. Besides, Aurora was now quite fond of Michael and thought him more handsome than her enchanted Prince.

"Yes, father, it's true," she admitted.

The King said to Michael, "Young man, you have done well. You may choose one of my daughters to be your wife. And someday, my kindgom will be yours."

Michael smiled at the two sets of twins. He smiled at the two sets of triplets, and he smiled at the youngest, the pretty Alicia. Then he chose Aurora for his wife.